Don't Take Your Snake for a Stroll

DON'T Take Your Snake for a Stroll

KARIN IRELAND   DAVID CATROW

HARCOURT, INC.   San Diego   New York   London   Printed in Singapore

If you take your pig out shopping,
Don't take him to the mall.
He'll play in the dirt in the planter outside
And you won't get to shop at all.

Don't take your elephant down to the beach,
No matter how much he begs.
After hours of rubbing on bottles of lotion,
You'll barely have covered his legs.

If you take your snake out for a slither,

Don't take it where others will be.

Small children will shriek, old ladies will faint,

And you'll headline the news on TV.

Don't let your chimp help you string Christmas lights,
Though you think she could do the job faster.
She could—but she'd do it by climbing the tree!
The result would be a disaster.

If you go to a dance, better go there alone.

Don't take your rabbit along.

You might want to cha-cha, you might want to waltz,

But she'll bunny-hop all night long.

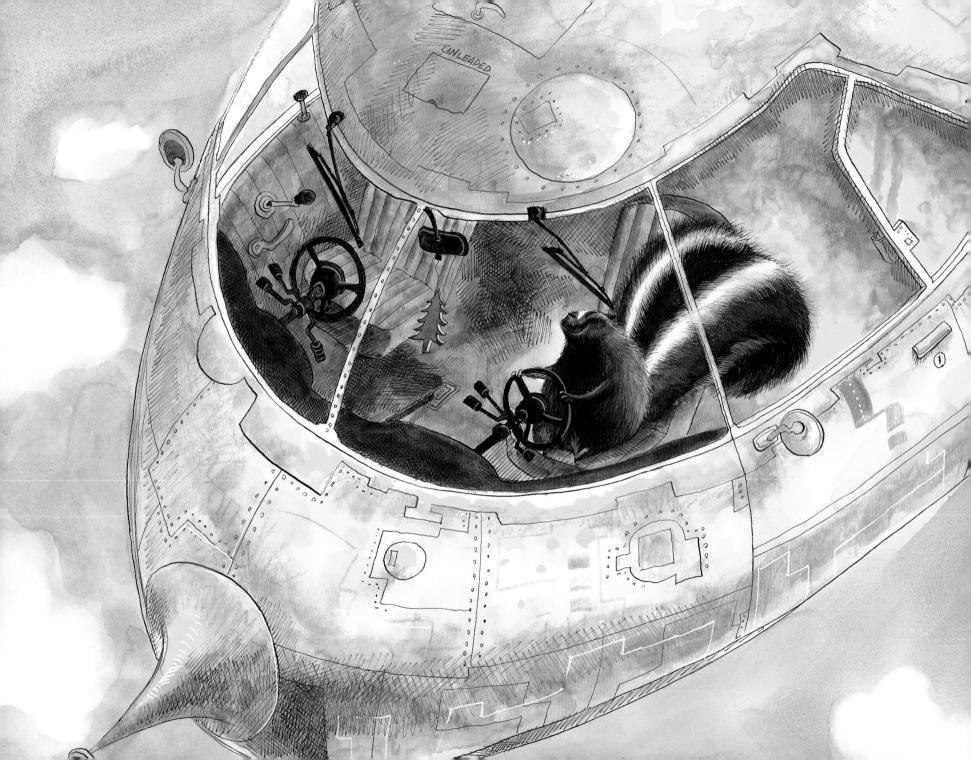

Don't take your skunk on an airplane.
He'd make some trouble, I think.
If the ride gets bumpy and he gets scared,
There could be a terrible stink!

Don't take your moose to the movies
When he says he would like to go.
The people behind him will wiggle and squirm,
But they won't see much of the show.

When you go out to dine on some fancy cuisine,
Don't let your frogs go there with you.
The waiters will think they've escaped from the chef
And a spirited chase will ensue.

Le Finger Dip

Don't take your duck to a wedding reception
Where punch is served in a fountain.
He'll take one look and jump in for a swim.
No, it's better you go there without him.

If you go on vacation, please go by yourself.

Don't bring along your kangaroo.

Moms carry their babies safe in a pouch,

And she might want to keep you there, too.

Don't take your coyote for a night on the town,
Especially when there's a full moon.
He'll howl and he'll yowl as loud as he can,
And he really can't carry a tune.

If you go to a swing-dance party,

Don't take your rhinoceros there.

She's as big as a truck and her clothes don't quite fit

And the guests are all likely to stare.

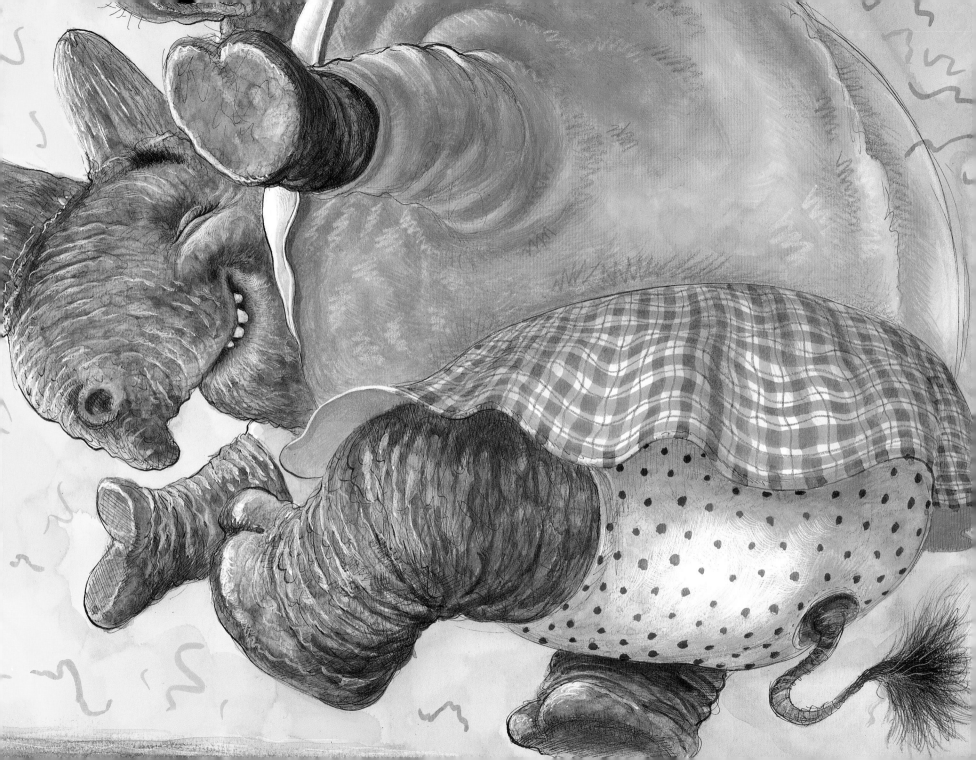

If you walk in the park at night before dinner,

Think twice before bringing your 'gator.

A lady once took hers out for a walk,

And her 'gator got hungry and ate her!

If you want to have fun without worry,
Listen to what you should do:
Leave all of the animals tucked in at home
And take only people with you.

For Tricia, as always,
and for Shane, you're the best,
and for Ireland Nelson Stirling, who is more wonderful than I have words for
—K. I.

For Dan, my little brother
—D. C.

www.HarcourtBooks.com

Library of Congress Cataloging-in-Publication Data
Ireland, Karin.
Don't take your snake for a stroll/by Karin Ireland; illustrated by David Catrow.
p. cm.
Summary: Mayhem ensues when a little boy takes unusual pets like a rhinoceros and a kangaroo to places usually reserved for people.
[1. Pets—Fiction. 2. Wild animals as pets—Fiction. 3. Stories in rhyme.] I. Catrow, David, ill. II. Title.
PZ8.3.I65Do   2003
[E]—dc21   2002003489
ISBN 0-15-202361-5

First edition
A C E G H F D B

The illustrations in this book were done in watercolor on bristol board.
The display type and text type were set in Opti Adrift.
Color separations by Colourscan Co. Pte. Ltd., Singapore
Printed and bound by Tien Wah Press, Singapore
This book was printed on totally chlorine-free Enso Stora Matte paper.
Production supervision by Sandra Grebenar and Ginger Boyer
Designed by Judythe Sieck